To Charlotte —

Warm purrs

Brian Hein

Published by Ballyhoo Books
P.O. Box 534
Shoreham, NY 11786

Copyright 2000 by Brian J. Heinz
Illustrations copyright 2000 by June H. Blair
Designed by June H. Blair

   Library of Congress Cataloging-in-Publication Data
Heinz, Brian J., 1946-
   The barnyard cat / Brian J. Heinz, author ; June H. Blair,   illustrator.
   p. cm.
   Summary: Barnabus, a seemingly lazy cat by day, proves himself invalu-
able to the farm by night as he defends the harvest grain against an army of
marauding rats.

   ISBN 0-936335-04-1 (hc.)
   [1. Cats--Fiction. 2. Rats--Fiction. 3. Farm life--Fiction.
   4. Stories in rhyme.] I. Blair, June H., 1949- ill. II. Title.

   PZ8.3.H41344 Bar 2000
   [E]--dc21

99-048768

   RL: 2.6
   Printed in China
   September 2000
   10 9 8 7 6 5 4 3 2

The farmboy shuts the corncrib door,
He locks the paddock gate,
And slams the shutters on the shed -
The hour's growing late.

Barnabus is dozing on a
Haystack in the sun.
He's belly up, his tongue is out,
His work has not begun.

For my niece, Moira 🐾 BJH

For Alfie...Mary· Stacey· Addam· Heath 🐾 JHB*

*The artist wishes to acknowledge the contribution of her parents' cats:
Stormin' Norman and Chip...as well as her own cat Foxy.

The Barnyard Cat

by Brian J. Heinz

Illustrated by June H. Blair

BALLYHOO BOOKS

Shoreham • New York

Barnabus, the barnyard cat,
Stretches toe to tail.

He springs atop the wagon seat
And down upon the pail.

Clover meadows, autumn-stilled,
Are draped in haunting shadows,
But raggle-taggle bands of rats
Are creeping in the hollows.

One by one these outlaws troop
With fierce and beady eyes.
They shuffle through the stubbled wheat
To steal the harvest prize.

Their leader is an ugly brute,
A hulking, rumpled beast.
His gaping snout and drooling jowls
Anticipate the feast.

Barnabus, unruffled, cranes his
Neck to sniff the air.
He smells the evil army and he
Races to prepare.

Over the tractor and into the mire,
Underneath the barrow,
He covers the ground in bounding strides,
A fleet-footed, fur-covered arrow.

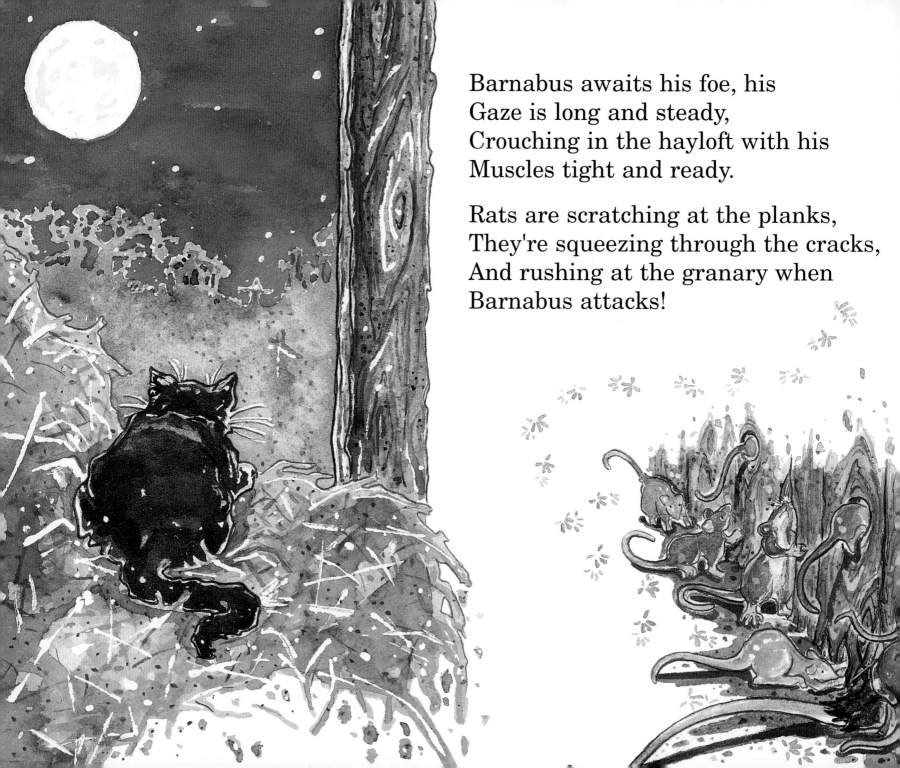

Barnabus awaits his foe, his
Gaze is long and steady,
Crouching in the hayloft with his
Muscles tight and ready.

Rats are scratching at the planks,
They're squeezing through the cracks,
And rushing at the granary when
Barnabus attacks!

Surprise!

Surprise in all the eyes of
Terror-stricken rodents,
The air-borne feline rockets down...
He relishes this moment.

Barnabus displays his weapons
Lit by lantern light.
The rats look to their leader...
Do we flee? Or do we fight?

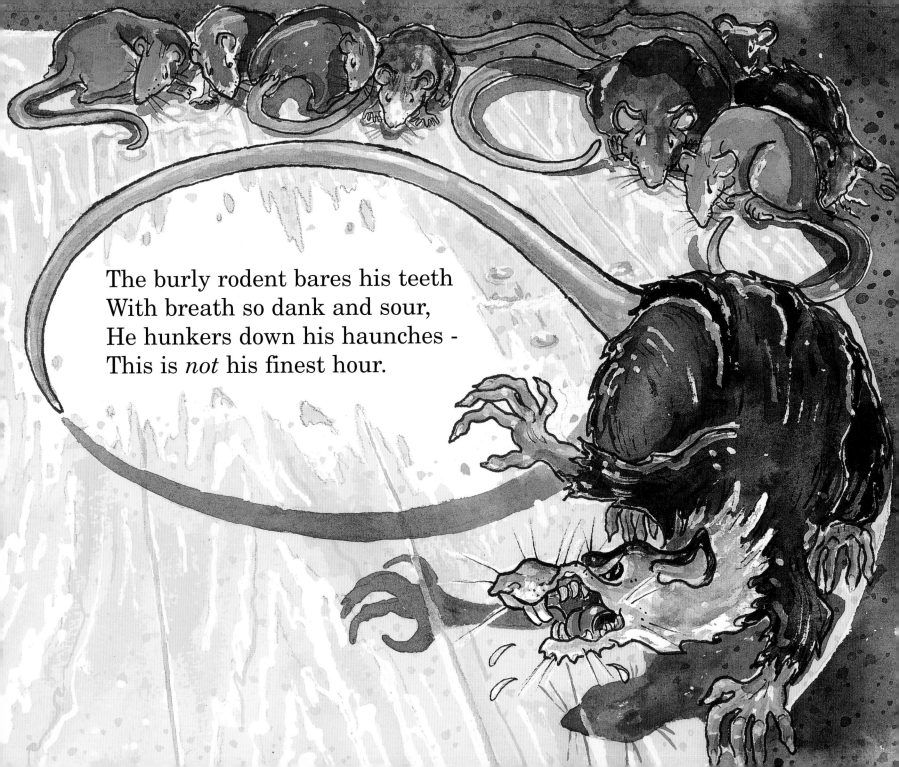

The burly rodent bares his teeth
With breath so dank and sour,
He hunkers down his haunches -
This is *not* his finest hour.

Barnabus extends his paw and
Swats the vermin's rump.
The rat goes reeling backwards
And the barn begins to jump.

Diving, gasping, panicked rats go
Scrambling up the stalls,
Or catapult from sleeping pigs
Through knotholes in the walls.

Rats between the pitchfork tines and
Leaping 'cross the bales,

With Barnabus in hot pursuit
Just inches from their tails!

It's **helter-skelter!**

Head for shelter,
Each and every one.

The rat race runs for hours...

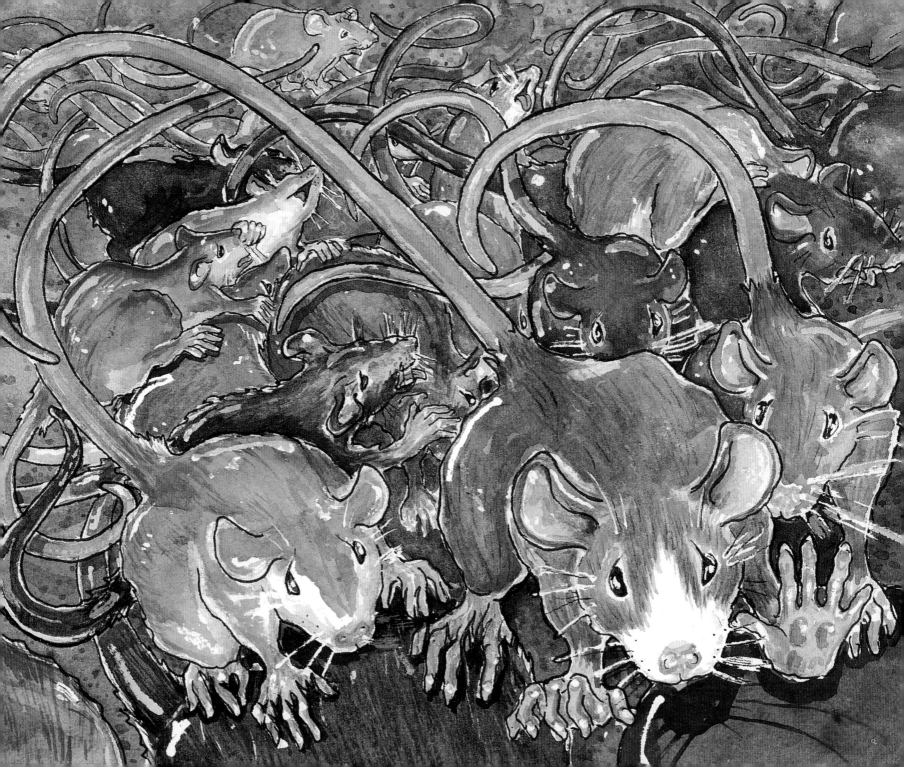

Past the scarecrows in the field,
They scurry in the night, but

Barnabus comes trotting home
At daybreak's welcome light.

Barnabus is dozing on a
Haystack in the sun.

He's belly up. His tongue is out
A good night's work is done.